About the Author

Born near Liverpool, **John Latham** has worked for over 40 years as a research scientist specialising in cloud formation. A recipient of several medals from the Royal Meteorological Society, he was, for eight years, president of the International Commission on Atmospheric Electricity, and founded the Atmospheric Physics Research Group at UMIST (which later became the University of Manchester's Centre for Atmospheric Science). In 1988 he moved to the US, to become a Senior Research Fellow at the National Centre for Atmospheric Research in Colorado.

Latham is the author of six collections of poetry, including *All-Clear* (Peterloo Poets, 1990) and *Sailor Boy* (The Collective Press, 2006), as well as short fiction, one novel – *Ditch-Crawl* (Comma, 2006) and several radio plays, broadcast on BBC Radio 4. His poetry has won first prize in over 20 competitions, and the title poem for his collection won second prize in the UK's 2006 National Poetry Competition.

Acknowledgements

Six poems in this collection ('The Artist is Not Satisfied', 'A Question of Dignity', 'Flood', Translation from the Latin', 'Secret Garden', and 'Green Wheelbarrow with Bright Red Stripes') first appeared in the pamphlet *Trench-Fever*, published by Mellen Poetry Press (New York, 1996). A version of 'Over the Hill, Still Far from Understanding' first appeared as 'Song-Snatches' in *Brando's Hat* (1988). Acknowledgements are due to the editors. The idea inspired by the conversation with the poet's son Mike, referred to in the poem 'Soggy Mirrors' (that spraying atomised seawater into ocean clouds would increase their reflectivity, and therefore may abate global warming) was first published in *Nature* ('Control of Global Warming?', 1990, #347, pp339-340).

By the same author

Unpacking Mr Jones
From the Other Side of the Street
All Clear
The Unbearable Weight of Mercury
Sailor Boy
Ditch-Crawl (a novel)

First published in Great Britain in 2017 by Comma Press
www.commapress.co.uk

ISBN: 978-1910974285
EAN: 978-1905583799

The publishers gratefully acknowledge assistance from the Arts Council England.

Supported using public funding by
ARTS COUNCIL
ENGLAND

Set in Bembo 11/13
Printed and bound in England by Clays

From Professor Murasaki's Notebooks on the Effects of Lightning on the Human Body

JOHN LATHAM

Contents

From Professor Murasaki's Notebooks on the Effects
    of Lightning on the Human Body   1
At the Morning Session on the Chemistry of Fog   3
Adiabatic   4
From *A Glossary of the Forms and Qualities of Ice*   5
The Artist is Not Satisfied   6
Rose–Blood   7
Zatopek   8
A Question of Dignity   10
Indian Summer   12
Bandaging   13
Chocolate Cake Lady   14
Valedictory   15
Translation from the Latin   18
Odd One Out   19
Breakfast Time   20
Two Telegrams   21
Untying   22
Over the Hill, Still Far from Understanding   23
House Not Listened To   24
Thirst   25
The Fallen Angel Sprawling at my Feet   26
Song Genesis   27
On Not Reading Barchester Towers   28
One Hundred Yard Dash   30
Soggy Mirrors   31
Beyond the Unnavigable Marsh   32

On Friday I'm to Rendezvous with Kathy C   47
Tutankhamun's Coppersmith   48
Silver Star for Being Good   50
Midnight Snap   52
Green Wheelbarrow with Bright Red Stripes   54
Secret Garden   55
Flood   56
The President's Tears   57
The Carbon Cycle   58
Hitler's Visits   59
Turning the Wireless Knob   60
Repairing the Jamworks Hoist   61
Ferrous Collage   63
Double-Jointed   65
Absinthe Drinker   67
The Attendance Register   71
Transatlantic Connection   73
Bodily   74

From Professor Murasaki's Notebooks on the Effects of Lightning on the Human Body

(Translation handwritten in margins, credited to N. Murasaki)

89. Incident on the Horikiko Coast (30/07/78)
Young couple alone, he recumbent on red rock
near pinnacle of sand-hill pocketed with grass,
she by his feet, sky making threat of raindrops
though earth remaindered dry. Mid-afternoon,
adjacent to sun's zenith, she touching ground
at plural potions of her body, while lightning
conflaged cracked dead-bush 6m from stone,
surge entering body by left toe and knee-skins
scorched but hardly. Consciousness abandoned
but resumed itself to her beyond thirty minutes
bequeathing no damage but burn marks, livid
at spine terminus, shaping like shouting throat.
Her memories of suction into light fibrillating
like new leaves. Man felt no perverse effects,
seven heart-flowers uncorrupted in his hand,
though since he suffers rapture of tympanum.

213. Higashi-Yuri-Machi Incident (22/09/97)
In Takaiwa-Yama, summer's declining parts,
school-teacher of language and nine-year son
relaxing in garden by lotus pool at light-fade,
playing go. No hailstones, no St. Elmo's Fire,
so foreboding invalid, yet flash strick jay-tree
20m distance, beneath whose roots iron pipe
reclined, convoying pool-water at arid times.
Predominant currents swept below go-board
and players either side, with subsidiary flow
up left leg of father, departing from his body
at index, central fingers of right hand almost

1

touching board. They badly cindered, fused,
yet still holding black stone for further play.
There is death in the ha-ne, as proverb says.
Boy hurtled into water, naked as carried out,
unscathed except for fern-prints on left heel.

At the Morning Session on the Chemistry of Fog

The head flung back above the chair in front of me
belongs to a woman I don't know. Someone
sneaks in late, and two of its hairs stir in the breeze.

Her brain is less than a foot away from mine,
and as Zen, from Kyoto, drones remorselessly on
about the scavenging of sulphur by dendritic ice

I long to tap some of its memories – not those
she hugs each night as her lover lies in sleep –
but faded ones she can no longer recollect

possibly pale milk-tastes from her first months,
haunting songs without an ending or a face,
someone sighing as a carriage pulls away.

These and others she allows me, though
she doesn't know or care. Dare I touch them?
Would they shrivel if I held them to the light?

To hell with coalescence by electrostatic forces,
I'm glimpsing something that could upturn my life
though it will not happen, and perhaps I'm glad.

I wonder if she's searching for unexacting love
which I seek too, but not from anyone alive
or lately dead. I feel safe now only in my dreams.

Not fair to linger with a mind so freely offered,
so I close my eyes, steer it into shade
and as Zen approaches climax, fold it in pale silk.

Adiabatic

I'm motionless, naked, lying on my side,
my knees drawn up, all of me underneath
the sheet, my arms tight across my chest,
toes curled. Motionless, my heart-beats
steady as the ocean, my eyes tight closed,
drifting through the dawn. I'm safe, alone,
not lonely. My fingers soften, pillow me.
I sink deeply home. No other life exists,
I want no-one, nothing, only now. I curl
my shoulders inwards, round my heart
and all its heat, my temperature steady,
a new plateau. I am adiabatic, complete.

From *A Glossary of the Forms and Qualities of Ice*

Tyndall flowers: Trapped inside ice, they drift implacably
from cool to warm, ghost-figures, petals ringed with light.
The inch-long journey takes a week. Switch temperatures,
they creep back again. They never wilt or lose composure.

Snowflake drowning: It jigs sideways, settles on a wave.
Its extremities melt before the body. Its cold water sinks
through brine nibbling at its surface, and starts to retract
into a sphere. Still intact, but soon to be dispersed forever.

Lightning trigger: In the cloud a hailstone bristles, distorts
electric force-lines, compresses them until stressed-out air
breaks down, a spark leaps out of ice, becomes a filament
glowing on its wayward path to earth. The sky cracks open.

Snow crystal history: Air temperature dictates its shape,
all six corners sprout. As winds swirl it round the cloud
it grows columnar, prismatic, dendritic in turn, the finest
details of its hour-long journey writ in ice: until the thaw.

Hoarfrost architecture: Under snow, ice crystals re-adjust,
create from chaos arrays of fluted columns, becoming frail,
stretched invisibly along the mountainside. Glittering city
in almost dark, until a falling stone creates an avalanche.

Pressure melting: A steel wire draped over an ice-block,
huge weight fastened to each end. Years before the wire
cuts through. As the weights crash to the cold-room floor
the ice-block shows no sign that anything has happened.

The Artist is Not Satisfied

She frowns, angles her brush to gauge perspective.

Something in his face she's failed to capture,
a freshness this second sitting
has destroyed - or possibly
those eyes hold something unexpected,
mockery, perhaps, an absence of control.

She mixes raw umber with cobalt blue.

Her first stroke sections him
left cheekbone to right forehead,
the second sponges out an eye. The next
obliterates the smile that makes her nervous.
Paint trickles from his mouth onto his shirt.

The brush collects a little crimson.

She wastes him, attacking from all sides,
gashes him until his face is blank,
he sinks into a pool of mud.
She feels for him below the surface,
stabbing, trepanning him: then leaves.

He stands on her side of the easel, shaking.

Rose–Blood

She's restless in this bed
she'll never leave.

Today I am her father
yesterday a man called Jake
I do not know.
Sometimes I am me.

As I turn her wrist towards me
trace its labyrinth of blue
I glimpse sunlight glinting
from the flower-garden below,

and I'm seventeen again
my arm snakes
from the hawthorn hedge,
offers her the rose.

But she doesn't move,
she's staring at a scarlet arc
deepening on my skin.
Beads well along its length,

she tongues one, swallows,
her lips limpet onto me.
She sucks each one
and all barriers, away.

She's resting now
but as I tiptoe to the door
a sleep-laced question
lassoes me, draws me back:

What's that thorny flower
that tastes of blood?

Zatopek

If you want a medal, sprint, he said. *But if you wish*
to know yourself, you must run a marathon.
In his golden years he almost never saw the soles
of other runners' shoes.
The post-war crowds, still nervous, starved,
found a hero they could love,
chant his name, three syllables:
Za-to-pek, Za-to-pek, Za-to-pek.
Head rolling, face contorted, pure agony,
he'd dig deep and even deeper,
accelerate his growing pain away,
lap his competitors,
though they were scarcely relevant to him.
His battle was always only with himself,
and now he's breasted the tape this final time.

She runs alone, eschewing company,
no crowds or clamour
she takes uncharted mountain trails,
loves their only sound, the crunch
of boots on snow. Or in summer, a sough,
as her feet draw fragrance
out of pine-needles. Most of all
she loves the early-morning fog,
through which she ghosts. Invisible, no trace.
She is at one with the woman
whose company she shares alone so rarely.
The silence speaks to her, no words
needed. She soaks it in,
welcomes everything around her,
rejoices in the harmony she feels.

A solitary hand-clap. A coyote's howl.
They pass each other, scarcely visible,
eyes touching for a moment
approving what they see, as slight
yet as important as a kiss.

A Question of Dignity

Silver-haired colossus
prophet's profile

he broods, furrowed
throughout the afternoon

unmoving, blank-faced.
When his daughter comes

her arms outstretched
her kisses fail to reach him.

She strokes his passive hand
walks reluctantly away.

And now, night ward
lit by one faint spot,

hours into his monologue
deep underground

his words
approximate as coal

come out of her trouble,
can't resurrect him now.

Rearing out of bed
silhouetted against sleep

his drip-frame a skeleton
tottering behind

standing, feet splayed,
back discreetly turned,

head bowed,
pissing on the floor.

Indian Summer

Blinks open to a dead man dancing.
Baggy pants, worn slippers, shirt
with faded blue-grey squares,
he's lurching to some music
which no-one else can hear
whose frayed edges whisper:
Enough! I've had enough. Yet,
his reeling has a clumsy grace
a shadow-waltz of stunted trees,
drunken barges singing.
Leaning to the mirror, his eyes
grow thirsty, huge. Angling back,
they wraith away. He sees what,
when she said it, he did not believe,
that he is beautiful, despite
his breathlessness, the tightness
in his head, his jaundiced skin.
He spins, though his loose heart
threatens to break free. She,
gliding from the silence, aches
into his eyes, aches into his eyes
until she sees he cannot stop.
So she joins him in the dance,
they whirl deep into green
touch everywhere before the drum.

Bandaging

Emily is carrying her daughter's wounded mind
through the village: her morning ritual.
She feels dizzy, stumbles, her eyes plead
with her neighbours not to help.

The mind has been bleeding in the cavities
of night, but now the stains are almost dry,
their fragrances, subdued, pink and lavender,
much older than unremembered life.

In Lupin Wood she uncovers lint and cotton,
blind fingers untying every knot. She lays it
in a moss-lined bowl scoured out of stone
by wind. It sighs as it sinks in.

She bathes it in mottled air and birdsong,
the thoughtful drip of water from tall trees.
Though she can't staunch new bleeding
she eases it with balm of chicory.

She leaves it sleeping, sets off light for home,
her feet attempt to skip. She'll harbour hope
until tonight, when muted weeping wakes her
and she slips into the dark to start again.

She no longer remembers her daughter's name,
the colour of her hair, her smell. She's not sure
if she still lives, was ever born.
All she knows is that bandaging is needed.

Chocolate Cake Lady

Why d'you call me 'Daddy', you who baked me cakes when I
    was small?
You, who loved rust's blemishes, its warmth: who breathed
on the lenses of your glasses
when you'd something difficult to say:
who gnawed your knuckle to the bone trying not to cry.

Somewhere a cat called Scraggs who licked varnish off the
    floor.
I'm sure I saw you coffined. How did you get out?
I do not mind, perhaps.
Your name has left me. Did we live together? Love?

Perhaps you're an amalgam. If so, it doesn't matter
which of you have died,
who stole the German microscope,
hid morphine from her father in extremis,
poured gin, one Sunday morning, in the holy water at St.
    John's.

When I licked the varnish, my mouth filled up with fluff.
Perhaps, in the end, you found a love outside of memory. I
    hope so.
I'm comfortable here, blanketed by soot,
an orchid growing where a quill of light sneaks through.

My father found him in a rusty rabbit trap – a cat called
    Scraggs.
Perhaps I'm not the I you know.
Your sorrows dim your lustre. Chocolate cake lady, let me be.

Valedictory

His sedative creates for him a five-hour sleep
which he can function on, though scarcely.
Today he allows himself a luxury, ten minutes
before rising from his bed. Time to search
for those dreams he can't remember, stretch
each arm and leg, each finger, toe, a thawing,
one by one, of his rigidities. Perhaps one day
he'll skip again, or even vault a fence, play
hopscotch in the street, though he's not seen
those chalked rectangles for sixty years or so.

But now he must focus on today. In two hours
he'll be confronting the audience, edgy silence
growing as they begin to wonder if he'll speak:
a game he'd loved, because it sucked them in,
emasculated them. But now, after his stroke,
his first lecture for years, perhaps the words
wont come, he'll hate the compassion rippling
round the room, the glee of old colleagues
who'd suffered from his lacerating tongue.

Surely he can do it one more time. He winks
at himself in the bedroom mirror. Oh yes,
he'll succeed, as always, his timing exact,
each sentence elegant and fluid, his ripostes
to every question urbane, polite, oblique,
yet devastating as his subtle words sink in.
He'll be dominant as ever, they'll clap on
until he raises a self-effacing hand. Then
he'll stand humbly at the lectern, affirmed.

His room troubles him. Why have his shoes
been polished, he wears only slippers now?

Whose are those stacked papers? That suit
is far too large, and he can't fasten his tie.
He recollects that he's to talk, but on what,
to whom, has slipped away. Terror mounts,
but he can't reveal his cowardice, not now.
And surely he was always fuelled by fear.
This, his final challenge. He'll relish it.
He winces, smiles at tapping on his door.

Translation from the Latin

The centurion is slaying the lion in the olive grove
while Nancy Cornes is waiting in Phipps Wood.
I wish the centurion would slay Old Fishwick
and the lion chew his stinking corpse to cud.

He thrusts his sword deep into its breast.
Not 'thrust' last Tuesday evening – more a judder
not 'breast' in the grass behind the palings
but fingers whose coolness made me shudder.

The beast was silenced in mid-roaring.
I wasn't, it came out a full-blown scream
while she made only a bubble-pop of sound
as if she'd glimpsed some magic by the stream.

The lion slumped, quivered and lay still.
I felt vanquished, as if I'd run a mile
while she knelt, hair tenting me, nestling
my wan shrinkage, lips flickering a smile.

He gazed with sorrow at the beauty of his foe.
Johnnie waves as he saunters to the wood.
I pray to God to smite him with green boils
and for Nancy to wait longer, as a lover should.

Odd One Out

They sit around the fire, a dozen boys
on a pentagon of logs, huddling close
as darkness thickens, shadows scud
across huge eyes and pallid limbs.

Cocoa, stories, songs. My nephew,
first night away from home,
beams at the stars, claps his hands,
bounces, shouts the words,

roars and stamps, not noticing
all other sounds have died.
Then his voice thins, wavers,
he's overshot again. But surely

it won't matter, he smiles around,
this tittering will die. It subsides
then someone grabs his glasses,
flips them high into the fire.

He washes in stream-water, unrolls
his sleeping bag, breaks down only
when a fat boy gives him toffee.
He weeps until they take him home.

That night his glasses writhe, beseech him
from the flames, shudder him awake.
She tries to quell his shaking, convince him
he's OK. She strokes him back to easy sleep.

On the wall above her, dozing by his bed,
a space-ship soars. A boy with glasses

piloting, a smiling passenger,
the caption, in blue crayon, *Me and Mum*.

Breakfast Time

I'm strapped into my high-chair,
my feet play hide-and-seek.
I'm banging on the polish
with a tooth-marked wooden stick.
A remorseless spoon is tracking me.
I shake my head so hard
my eyeballs fill with stars
but it dodges past my fingers,
tips porridge in my mouth.
I yell, and in it comes again.
I try to spit it out
but choke on it and swallow.
Good boy, she smiles,
rises from her knees, spins
multi-coloured beads along my rail.

Two Telegrams

l. (1944)

I skip into the wash-house, find my mother
and my aunt, arms wrapped around
each other, their wailing up and down
like the air-raid warning siren, last night.
Is the pool spreading across the concrete
floor made out of tears? Telegram floating
on the water, but I'm afraid to pick it up.
They spot me, draw me into them,
bosoms, helpless, pressed into my face.
Suffocating, terrified, over-spilling sink.
They keep calling *Tommy, Tommy,*
and I call too. But Tommy doesn't come.

ll. (1961)

An unopened telegram, sent 50 years ago,
5.44pm on the day before my wedding.
All forgiven. Every joy to you. Veronica.
Who? I'm bewildered, but as the day
wears on, faint echoes. Chance meeting,
cinema, back row, our hand-clasp easy,
slowly growing fierce, nails digging in,
a wanted pain. I seek more but she uncoils,
whispers: *Too soon. Let's take our time.*
Outside, she tugs my hand: *Let's go!*
I long to, but must tell her of tomorrow.
She swallows, *Shame!,* walks off into the fog.

Untying

He sits at the mirror, winds the silk
around his neck, holds the thin end
taut, loops it with the thick,
pulls through. Untied, it slips again
onto the floor. Another simple task
for sixty years becomes impossible.
He sees panic flicker round his eyes.

Hold your chin up, love! Recollects
the day he started school, starched
shirt, blazer, freshly cobbled shoes.
Her fingers brush his throat
as she twirls the tie and knots it,
a skill like riding two-wheeled bikes,
he knows he'll never have.

The woman in white kneels to him
and ties it, skin warm as his mother's,
same solicitude. He tries to explain
it's different in the mirror: *Think
about it, and it can't be done.*
He tries but the words won't come,
won't ever come to him again.

Did she know he unfastened his top button
each morning on his winding way to school?

Over the Hill, Still Far from Understanding

No need to draw a blade across your wrists. If the pen
clipped to your pocket jabs into your eye, fling it away.

How can you write the smell of cellars, a sunset
glimpsed while drowning, the pucker of a baby's lips?

Still the barnacles sing, mariners' rib-cages rattle,
no-one in the upper street has slippers made for dancing,
a good wife strokes the photo hidden in her locket

and in the leaf of morning, eyelids drooped with dew,
Mary parts the bracken for her missing shoe

and when drum-beats fade, her throat is clogged with ash,
no-one on the island will remember the acid taste of green.

God help you, son, the old stones mutter.

Mutter, mutter meine, come back out of the winds
that long dispersed you, nourish me again,
tell me tales of simple times, before the flood,
the flow of blood, the parchment.

Then, I'll slip foxgloves on my fingers,
slither through wild diamonds to the far side of the hill,
crawl into my barrel, tap the chocks away.

House Not Listened To

Its shape looms out of grey,
familiar, I do not know.
I lunge, grasp brittle ivy
that wreathes its southern face,
hang on against the pull, haul in.

This house has not been listened to.

I kneel and rest my ear
against its chimney-breast,
learn its breathing's roughness,
pipes weeping at the joints,
shuddering of unswept soot.

Knots in the beams
make strangely angled faces,
paint-blisters have lost pressure,
none of the doors quite fit.
I call: *Can I move in?*

I promise to be a good physician.
My finger is learning how to talk,
writing words on cellar walls,
words not found in books
but in the dictionary of the heart.

This time I won't hover
in the shaded doorways,
I'll dance the tattered carpets,
dream in every room,
let each room sleep in me.

Tell me. Can I move back in?

24

Thirst

It rounds the corner, sweeps
towards the edge,
bearing foam-flecks, bubbles,
a maple leaf, a twig.

Its silence sucks on him
invites him in,
he clasps the iron railing
longing to leave go.

If so, would it succour him,
absorb his pain
return him
to the anonymity of dark?

Would he feel comforted
as gravity takes over,
and he plunges, full of wonder
to white-capped rocks below?

The Fallen Angel Sprawling at my Feet

is coming round. She giggles
as my tweezers pick out grit
between her toes, sighs
as I sponge her feet with milk.
I slip sandals on her feet
– buckles magnify my need.
When I ask if she's my mother
she whispers: *Close your eyes.*
She's hovering, her feathers
tease my throat. Dangling free
I age, while dunes glide past
and the cavern breathes
in thoughtful candle-light.

Song Genesis
For Willy Russell

You took my page-locked poem
and in a flame-lit, wine-glow hour
plucked melody and beat

out of the fibrillating air,
coaxed, drummed, teased
massaged my errant words

until the room was singing.
No, you said, *not mine.*
The song was there already.

No more than David, crouching
in a marble block
until a chisel set him free,

or Uncle Vanya fretting
in a lofty drawing room
before a quill unlocked the door,

or the Law of Gravitation
lying dormant in an apple
until cold passion weighed its fall.

Our voices, noosed
by the strings of your guitar,
uplift into a January sky.

Perhaps the song is always there already.

On Not Reading Barchester Towers

My truest friends or alter egos are characters in books,
available whenever I'm in need. If I want to ache
with laughter until all woes are gone, I make my way
to old St Petersburg, where Marmeladov turns it on.
For solace I smoke a pipe with Huck: we do not speak.
If I need a frank opinion I seek out Joe Gargery, who
unlaces his great boots to help him think. For wildness,
abandonment, I send a carriage for Nastasya Filippovna,
her dance transfixing everyone before she sweeps away.
So many I've not met. But my time has almost gone.
Do I hunt again with Levin, sport with Molly Bloom,
revisit these old friendships or search for different ones?

Not just people, places they inhabit. Even from this bed
my body's trapped in now, I can listen to soft groaning
in morning mists on Borodino's battle-field, clamber
over ivy, gigantic slates on the roofs of Gormenghast,
crouch, praying, in a classroom cupboard while a man
flexes his cane, drools, calls out my name. I've been lost
inside a hayrick, five blind kittens my only company.
I've meandered ancient moors in lashing rain, sat inside
an Irish pub, marvelling that everyone is beautiful in song,
lingered at a Russian railway station, hoping to save her
if she jumps. I'd take her to Yoknapatawpha County
and richness of language would speed her convalescence
as she and a damaged boy console each other in their loss.

Sonja swirls into my party, crystals spurting from her skates,
curtseys to K creeping sideways from my shoe. Vicious night
outside, mulled wine goes down well. Lebedyev sips slyly
from the holy water, Myshkin bathes Little Nell in milk.
Emma and Bathsheba swap husbands in a corner, Natasha
wraps a shawl around the shaking Quilp. Stephen Dedalus

arm-wrestles with Heathcliff. Oskar's drumming rises
to crescendo, shatters Mrs Gamp's *pince-nez*. Darl joins in
the madrigals, Fanny sautees fish. The fog is growing thick.
Polly Garter bites my ear, whispers *Call me Ishmael*. Dmitri
knits a cardigan for Mrs Dalloway. Clea weaves between us,
welcoming, chastising. She says a Mrs Proudie wants to join
my party. I've not met her, there's no time. Sadly, I say no.

One Hundred Yard Dash

Pale boy surging as the whistle blows.
Shirt billowing, he sprints ahead.
But those chest-pains seize him,
drag him down and out. He gasps
for air. He thumps the ground.

Hard youth strutting around
a midnight town, staggering,
two fingers jerked against the sky.
Nothing will deflect him, slow him
down. Nothing he will not try.

Young man lolling on an old armchair.
he's quiet, half-smiling, easy.
Not struggling for breath,
his white shirt shows no motion.
Perhaps he's unaware the race is over.

Soggy Mirrors
For Mike

He's ten years old, we've climbed Moel Eilio today,
we look out over Caernarfon, the Irish Sea, to a sky
on fire, thin stratus flaunting colour. He nudges me
and points: *Dad! Those clouds. Why do they shine?*
I tell him they're made of tiny water drops, millions,
even billions, bouncing sunlight back towards the sky.

Again I'm on the summit, four decades on, scarlets
just as vivid, clouds as shallow, shiny as before. But
he's not here, the silence is oppressive. He drifted
away into an early sunset, unknowing, no farewell.
I can almost conjure his asthmatic voice as he turned
to me and laughed: *Those clouds are soggy mirrors!*

Beyond the Unnavigable Marsh

*[It is not clear whether these exchanges were authored by one person
or two, though the handwriting points towards the former,
as does the location of the bones].*

1. Blue

Her fingers, sifting sand
close on broken glass
stained by ultra-violet

she squeezes it
holds it to the sun

it sucks her deep
into a flame-nest
cooler than the sky
down until she's floating
in a lake of helium

where everything is blue

even blood congealing
on her lacerated hand
pain, her missing name
the throbbing.

Even the taste of water
tilted to her lips

touch of hands
on the edge of memory

even the fears
she's forced to swallow.

2. Dandelions

They fill the canyon, loosely bobbing
veined in shadow
featureless in sun.

What time is it?

He rushes at them, cheeks puffed out
they glide aside
reconvene behind him.

If he could lie down gently
he'd float on them
not touching
sail trees' unseen spaces
drift fingers
over markings high on cliffs
listen to the trickle
of water over rock
where seepages
feed brooks that feed the lake.

What time is it?

He sucks them in
they clog his mouth until he chokes.

Levitated, glowing,
barbs and arrows
smothered by pure white
he glides into a tideless sea
where nothing moves
no sound exists

except from the far distance
a waft of breath, an echo.

They fill the canyon, loosely bobbing.

3. Bluebells

At first, scents wafting
from the bluebell grove
were too subtle to draw her
off the beaten track
though sometimes she'd skip
as if the sun had just come out.

But now, flowers luscious
after years of fallen leaves
heady fragrance tugs her
stumbling off course
she sinks into a hollow,
breathes bluebells in her sleep.

4. Blackberries

Forever on the cliff-edge, safely roped
he peers from clear light into shadow
stretches to the topmost fruit
finger-skates its blush
savouring its fragrance
tantalised by deeper berries
succulent, just out of reach below.

He sprawls in harvest, juices spurting
lips bruised, shaken by his fall,
squeezes, swallows
fills every cleft with flesh
welcoming the night's dark throat
sucking him away, lost at last
in a canyon clogged with blackberries.

5. Bougainvillea

She stares into the water.

Bougainvillea's shadow
shawls her paleness
her outstretched hands
the darkness of her hair

she could love this woman

leaves settle in the water
ripples lick and nibble
wash across her skin
her thighs squeeze tight

she can taste this woman

she kneels, lips swollen
peers into the water
searching for her face

she must mend this woman

lodged in upper branches
of the bougainvillea
an oval, eyeless
stretched into a howl

she slides into the pool.

6. Fissure

Half-way up the fissure
wedged between a boulder
and a toe-wide crack
he steers his head
towards the slice of sky

blinking spray
from slow drops
deadening his forehead
he sees it, high above him
– alpine columbine –

its blue, translucent
haloed by the sun
the only life and colour
in this world
of weeping rock

scuffed, slipping
he inches up
the climb impossible
except with pitons
which he spurns

plunges into blackness
he'll rise from
bruised and bleeding
time and time again
towards the columbine.

7. The Meadow of Immaculate Flowers

Stumbling the meadow of immaculate flowers
drunk with their fragrance
she kneels to the most beautiful of all

cups her hands to shield it from the sun
slakes its thirst with water
strokes its petals, whispers it to sleep

panics as it opens to her, blunders on
drunk with its fragrance
until she sees the most beautiful of all

kneels, hands cupped, shielding it from sun
slakes its thirst with water
strokes its petals, whispers it to sleep

panics as it opens to her, stumbles on
saddened by the weeping
until she sees the most beautiful of all.

8. Lilac

He glides around a frozen lake
ice a mirror
to the lilac sun
his shadow swift
free-wheeling
as he pirouettes
his skates' spume
patterning the colours
pattering the ceiling
over sluggish salamander,
lake extending
from oblivion to glory.

Silence resurrecting
a figure, torn
slow-sweeping,
skates day-dreaming
as she spirals in and out,
arms searching for him
in the shifting dark
intersecting his past
and future tracks
straining for him
as he slides away
dodging fiercely when she lunges.

9. Wounded Ruby

He'd take me on his knee
blow love-rings in my ears
raspberry the undersides
of my trapped feet
until my laughter shrilled
to shatter mirrors.
He'd set me on his knee again
hug me to his hugeness
whisper love-rings in my ears.

Story over, kissed goodnight,
he'd slide into my sheets
raise a tent for us
to play in pillow light
the game, to lie quietly
and never, ever smile
as in turn we took a feather
meandering for jewels.

If I found his wounded ruby
he'd give me sweets to suck
when I winced during his journey
through the grove of emeralds
his *You don't love me* made me cry.

10. Marigolds

Spring subdues his journey's bruises
broth trickle-feeds his strength

snow-melt sluices poisons
sorrel balms his wounds

night-frenzies
kaleidoscope to sleep.

Wakenings no longer fly the flags
of inner bleedings

he ripens in an orange haze
strolls through marigolds.

Meandering the valley's lip
he sees a distant storm

seethe, shudder
ripped by lightning's steel.

Its downwash chills him
he bites his knuckles, hard,

kicks away his shoes
tears off all his bandages

sprints towards the violence
arms outstretched, hair streaming.

11. Velvet Glade

She slips out of her clothes
enters a green avenue
creepers hanging soft
from every tree

sleep-walks into them
they stroke her as she knew
slow across all skin of her
her flesh begins to glow

eyes closed, motionless
she opens to their feathering
they play with her, slide over her
invade her every part

she's teased into a song
she loves to sing and hates to sing
it builds into a scream
flocks of parakeets rise.

Released at last, she dozes, calms
strolls a velvet glade
arms lifted to the sun,
spots a shaded side-path, swallows

slips off all her clothes
sleepwalks a green avenue
creepers hanging soft
from every tree.

12. Mrs Campion

I ask my mother: *Was my birth a hard one?*

She straightens from her washing basket,
swishes shrouds of steam
over dewdrops on the grass
pegs a shirt so hard it winces:
I knew all that schooling
would teach you dirty talk.

I ask Mrs Campion: *Was my birth a hard one?*
Her knife muses above the rhubarb pie
sinks into its crust,
cloves and coriander swathe her in their scents:
Tha fought all day to stay in't dark
you nearly didn't come.
She never let him in again.

Apple-cider, as she passes me the glass
darkens her wrist's purple.
So long ago, lad. Let it be.

13. Classy Puppet

Such a classy puppet
so finely tuned,
I knew my master's wishes
before he did,
my dance a mirror
to his every mood
reshaping them. Sometimes
I'd spice my pirouette
with faint impertinence,
enough to make him frown
or scratch his head.

These victories too small
to sponge away my hate
he'd make me moan at will
my legs high-kick
when all I wanted was to sleep.
He'd split me up
no parts in harmony,
dissolved.

I tried to drown,
I sought dismemberment by sharks.

14. Window

At a tall window, looking steeply down
my house yet not my house
strewn with family that once was mine
or almost mine
though when I do not know.
My youngest child
behind a mask of porcelain
tears coursing her crevices
white pimples, no living human face.
Her brother, arm consoling
ushers me away.

Thin window, looking steeply down
river rushing along the narrow street
whitecaps over carriages
but I am safe.
It climbs between the houses
waves rear, spurt.
Hissing chills my cheek
but I am safe,
with the family, mine
I do not know.
Water buffets walls, pours down glass,
the breakers surge.
Their undersides are thirsting.

Eyes touch in the deluge,
arms wave farewell,
all will be destroyed
except for me, safe
who is not there, was never there
forever dry
at some tall, thin window looking down.

On Friday I'm to Rendezvous with Kathy C

whom I don't remember, from our course
ten years ago, who wrote for a reference
which – studded with superlatives –
I sent off to the college straight away:
though still I couldn't place her
despite the poems she mailed me
which I read but didn't understand.
And she said yes to my suggestion
that we meet up in November
when I visit Oxford for a day. Kathy C
with whom perhaps I've made love often
in the scarlet languor of my solitary bed.
And it was good, though I don't know yet
if her hair is light or dark, if she likes
to skate the topography of shoulders,
drink Merlot, take persimmon in her tea.

I fear our evening will be polite and stilted,
with frequent furtive glances at the clock.
And as it creeps towards its closure,
dissolution of my dream, I'll blurt out
that I'm longing to sleep with her again.
She'll take my hand and swallow twice,
look coolly through my fever and say: *What?*

Tutankhamun's Coppersmith

Sand saltates around the pyramid
but no movement in this tomb,
no molecules of air
have stuttered in or out,
no detectable percussion
for three thousand years,
since the trumpet lying with him
was last played,
since the final thread of flesh
slipped off the bone.
A hundred generations
in all parts of the world
have come, fought, blossomed,
disappeared, leaving no trace.
But in this cosmic silence
heart-beats have not throbbed,
no memories trawled or stored,
nothing has taken place, except
the decomposition of the King.

Yet, there is evidence of dreams.
Could the artist have created
such noble curvature
if he'd not lain on straw
under an ever-shifting moon,
cupping the trumpet in his mind,
stroking, moulding it,
into shapes he had imagined
were fit for a dead King?
To seal his satisfaction
he impressed his fingerprints
on the shyest, unseen places
of his art. It lay untouched

for three millennia
until tonight, when its notes
were resurrected,
ghosting round the world,
and a billion people shivered
at the sound of their own mortality.

Silver Star for Being Good

She lifted me from nightmares
enfolded me
until my breathing slowed to hers.

She, the village illegitimate,
abandoned, four days old,
who never knew a mother's arms,

felt a man's rough face,
or smelled his sweat,
until two decades and my father.

Schooled throughout her girlhood
to curtsey to her betters
keep her inkwell clean

do what she was told
never what she was not.
Each week she won a silver star,

fending off the spectre, defect
of her blood, that would gobble her
if she relaxed and was not good.

Even now, at eighty, she'd shrink
with shame, if she thought
her children knew her story.

No wonder it was hard to let us go,
kneeling, soaping limbs, as far
as we'd allow into our teens,

stroking him through his long coma
eyes drilling through his blindness,
willing him to live,

her fear, as one by one we left her,
not for her new abandonments
but ours, to brittle light, uncertain dark.

Midnight Snap

In cloud, a mile above the dormant Earth
the air is stretched to snapping point.
Ice crystals and hailstones hiss, scar, spit
as they slide across each other, leap apart.
A sparrow sucked into an updraught
burns coolly in St Elmo's Fire.

Below, a man leans on a five-barred gate
whose knots, veins, creakings
he's known for fifty years,
in darkness and in light. He's trying
to subdue the thumping of his heart,
accept the doctor's verdict on his wife.

A girl kneels to a tree-stump
a hundred yards away, head bowed,
hair flaring to the grass.
Her rapture absolute, she's motionless
except for sporadic swallowing.
Her nails dig deep into her palms.

Unzipped, air inside the cloud goes wild.
A streamer crackles an erratic path
through shafts of melting hail
towards the Earth's dark bulk below.
A sheath of flame leaps up to meet it,
the countryside transfixed in violet light.

A squirrel jabbers at the thunderclaps,
the old man burrows deep into his past.
The kneeling girl is soothed
by the ancient smell of ozone. The sky

mutters and grumbles, rain torrential now.
Smoke rising from a stricken elm subsides.

Green Wheelbarrow with Bright Red Stripes

Every autumn he wire-brushed, sand-papered it,
varnished the new coats of green and red,
each day trundling it around the village square

reigning back against the slope on Sandy Lane,
his shoulders tilted to compensate for camber,
easing over cobbles, shielding it from rain,

talking softly to his mother all the time
rearranging cushions to ease her ride,
in winter tucking blankets round her feet.

Shell-shocked in the war, they said, pushing
a green wheelbarrow with bright red stripes,
and I saw that what seemed empty might be full.

Secret Garden

Six feet underneath the rhododendron bush
he planted fifty years ago,
curled on bracken, crackling as he turns,
he squints through cracked bamboo
at swallows slicing blue, inhales
through it the decadence of autumn.

He ponders the firm qualities of trees:
the dignity of sick elms
groaning only in their sleep,
coquettishness of saplings in a storm,
the intransigence of oaks
still standing to attention after death.

Shelter fashioned out of pick and shovel,
roof he constructed from a barrel's hoops,
his potato fingers that know soil's vagaries,
their prints worn almost to invisibility,
whose touch upon a stem or nervous leaf
is as diffident and gentle as a lover's.

Oil-lamp blackening puzzled roots above,
tobacco pouch, a loaf of bread,
scuffed boots, a cheese, a ball of twine,
a scatterbox of seeds, a turfing knife,
an angled iron stave
from which fresh-water drips into a jug.

He listens to soil's sleeplessness
earthworms gravely dance,
litanies of night-wind over leaves.
He snuffs the flame, plugs the bamboo,
and as the light subsides, the presence
of someone he once knew grows strong.

Flood

Her first visit to him, a week after he left,
crashing gears at the image in his mirror
of her face pressed against the window,
doll dangling, her goodbye wave still-born.
Not cried, her mother said over the phone
but every night since then she's wet her bed.

She bustles in, shoos him back, gives him
slippers and a newspaper: *I've come to clean
the house for you.* She dons her apron
and for hours she sweeps, scrubs, polishes,
serves him biscuits, cups of tepid tea.
She won't stop to play their special games.

He's dozing when the first drops splat onto
the kitchen floor, patter from the ceiling
and soon a stream is flowing. He curses,
races past her – dusting on the stairs –
to the overflowing sink, turns off the tap.
He sags, forehead pressed against the wall.

She's in the doorway, moist-eyed, thumb
in mouth. Six years old, she looks so small.
He sweeps her up and hugs her. She sobs:
It's all my fault. I want you to be happy.
She calms at last, pulls my ear to her lips,
whispers: *Daddy, I want you to come home.*

The President's Tears

I've no doubt that they were genuine,
your sorrow deep and real,
a father yourself, wanting to help.
I'm sure your words assisted many.

But how do you feel, each time
a drone you authorised
dips down, explodes, into a group
of mothers ten thousand miles away?

One blinks back into consciousness
finds a severed foot, wearing
a baby-shoe she'd laced an hour ago.
Another spots a tiny pyramid of brains,

scoops them up and cradles them,
still warm. She hums to them
and wonders if any of its thoughts
and joyous memories remain.

How do you feel, Mr President,
kind man you seem to be?
Can you extend your range
of love and grief a little further?

The Carbon Cycle

This man was modern once
though pre-biotic now
cindered, carbonised
not smiling but astonished
as his fluids are sucked
out of his truck into the sun

a pioneer
if our leaders have their way
the first of a nation
of charcoal figurines.

A dancing girl, a man at prayer,
a woman deep in childbirth
a boy, hunched over
what might have been a book

each revealing, by curvature
of hand, throat's tension,
brow's furrow, shoulder's slant,
what they felt
in that last moment
before their flesh was alchemised.

Hitler's Visits

I knew we'd win the war because the grocer said so,
Mr Lawless, best at sums in the whole world,
whose podgy fingers made me dizzy as they sped,
unerring, down my mother's list of groceries.
But what if Mr Hitler fled, went into hiding,
in the hidden forest that stretches round the world,
shaved off his moustache, pretended
to be dumb, and is hiding now on Frodsham Hill?
Each night he sneaks down to the village, sniffs
the blistered sausages my mother cooks for tea,
then climbs in through a window, hides upstairs,
and if I set off for the bathroom, he'll jump on me,
slice me with his swastika, make sausage-meat of me.
But I'm in bed, in agony, my bladder bursting,
I must act. What shall I do? Explode or be eaten?
And the wind is screeching. Hitler must be close,
I can hear his jack-boots scraping on the wall.
I no longer mind that I share my bed with Geoff,
he likes my made-up stories, he keeps me warm,
and now I understand how he can save my life.
No way can I venture from our bed into the dark,
so I pee, softly, on my brother, sound asleep.
I shout to my mother: *Mum! Geoff's wet the bed.*
She sprints upstairs, smothers him with kisses,
sponges him and finds a pair of clean pajamas.
No scolding, she rocks him until he sleeps again.
She hugs me, whispers: *You're a fine big brother.*
I smile, rejoice. Hitler has been thwarted once again.

Turning the Wireless Knob

It didn't happen often, at most three times a year,
but I loved it when, not long before the dawn,
he crept into my bedroom, squeezed my knee,
whispered: *It's time, but don't wake Geoff.*
We'd tiptoe downstairs, close the parlour door,
he'd resurrect the fire, unscrew a flask of tea,
we'd huddle round the wireless. He was mine.
He let me turn the handle, we zoomed on and on,
talk-song snatches from all around the world,
words I'd never heard, I was traveling with him,
I wanted nothing more, but he raised his finger
and we stopped five thousand miles from home,
in Madison Square Gardens – America, he said,
two men were just about to fight. Strange names
like Tami Maurielo, Gus Lesnevich, Joe Louis,
Ezzard Charles and Billy Conn. I didn't care
about the boxing, they kept feinting all the time.
My dad could have bashed them all one-handed,
but he wasn't there, he was smiling down at me.
I felt big and small, somewhat sad yet happy.
We sipped our tea, light slipped into the room,
I lay against his shoulder while he poked
the fire, and wild sparks scuttled out of sight.
I heard Mum in the kitchen, trying to be quiet,
she didn't join us, she knew this was our time.
But when I asked her later why she didn't come,
She smiled: *No point. That Joe Louis always won.*

Repairing the Jamworks Hoist

I'm cheesed off with my dad. Ruined my weekend. Who
  cares
if those crates of marmalade and jam stay down here
'til Monday, instead of four floors up?

Cheering from the soccer pitch. I bet spotty Dirk has scored
  again.
He'll be racing round the field, arms outstretched, dipping to
  the left
then to the right. *Show-off! Nowhere near as good as me.*

I'm in the loft, high as the church steeple, my dad tiny down
  below.
He waves, I ignore him. I don't want to help. I can see the
  game
from here. Spotty volleys home, starts strutting.

Dad shouts again. Still I take no notice. I snigger. Serves him
  right.
Listen lad, I'm testing. I want to see if the hoist will take my weight.
When I call again press hard on that green button. OK?

A steam-train blows its whistle, sets off from the station. I
  love
its chugging, the hooter's wail, great steam-puffs swelling
as they rise towards the sky.

For God's sake press the button and lower me down, you clown!
I whirl round. He's three yards away, hanging by one hand
from an iron hook, sixty feet above the ground.

I thump the green button. His descent is slow. As he spins I
  notice

how white his knuckles are. I scurry, weeping, down the stairs.
He drops nimbly to the ground, grins down at me: *Let's call it
quits!*

Ferrous Collage

When my grandad told me stories of his youth, in that
    Cheshire brogue that smelled of loam,
I was the child that he had been, and so my life began fifty
    years before my birth.

Today, as I move closer to my terminus, I gather items from a
    century ago,
start to assemble them, fashion a collage.

Iron warmed his spirit as he trudged through snow to school,
past pointed railings, a team of standing horses, the blacksmith's
    forge.
Snowing hard, hot potato in each pocket,
he – time-monitor, ten years old – must get there early
to wind up the great weights, pitted iron, of the clock
that had ticked two centuries away. As he told his story
I could hear that tick, watch the pendulum's incessant to and
    fro.

The school is long demolished, all its iron skinned with brown,
so today I'm making a collage composed of rust.

Its background a wooden book-crate's lid, screwed to the wall.
Aged to greyness, knotted, flawed, its stenciled letters, symbols,
almost faded away. Fastened to it, items cloaked with rust:
a horse-shoe with three broken nails; key for some great lock;
a butcher's bone-axe; 25-ounce weight, hexagonal; a groat;
half-inch spanner; broken metronome; fob-watch's skeleton;
hinges that will never creak again.

Looped around two nails a rusty iron chain – the sagging
in between a precise parabola. In dim light I beam it from the
    side.

Its shadow has a curvature I've never seen before.
Making a collage, but I am rusting now. My skin blotched, coarse.
Whatever clarity I had, and nearly all my memories, have gone.
Or perhaps they're buried deeper than my rusty spade can dig.

I'm following the path he took a hundred years ago. I've no wish
to change this route. It feels natural to sink back into childhood,
meander daisied fields, hum songs whose words I don't remember now.

Double-Jointed

Transcontinental day, but I'm back now
in the Rockies,
a spurting, crackling fire
sends flame-shadows scudding
round stripped-log cabin walls,
and a focused light up high, outside,
shows us snowflakes whirling,
crazy-dancing into oblivion.
We, five of us, old friends,
and a soft-voiced younger woman
who lives deep into the forest
and opens now a slender tin,
takes out a joint and lights it,
and as it slowly circulates
snowflakes swell, fall upwards.
The McGarrigles' loss-singing
moistens our wide eyes,
we drift from chairs onto the floor,
the fire's above me now,
I watch it through closed eyes
so I can't tell whose cool fingers
start to stroke my wrist, my palm,
and I don't need to know.
I simply want to savour
what will not occur again,
but this person knows me better
than I do myself. I'm engulfed.
Excitement starts to rise, I wonder
who it is – I hope the woman
from the forest, but I won't mind
if it's Kathy, I'd hate it to be Fred,
and now I'm desperate,
in ecstasy, I have to know, I force

my eyes to open, the room is full
of shadows, recalcitrant umbrellas,
and I see that I'm being stroked by me.

Absinthe Drinker

He's still brooding after eighty years
eyes veiled in some dark tent.
Forehead pale, palm buttressing his chin
but something now is different.

Then I was a student, solitary, lost.
He fascinated me. Windswept, on the brink
above a seething sea, he'd dive,
not caring if he'd sink.

Now he seems callow, while I've coarsened,
learned to compromise and grieve:
expect no more of life than a shared sunset
or a hand brushing my sleeve.

My son had the same spirit,
anarchic, reckless, bold,
consequences never weighed
and neither of them will grow old.

Jerfal

I have a choice to make. Keep my candle lit and see what a
    camera might see;
blow it out and see what a camera could not. I choose the
    latter.

The throbbing more pronounced, drum-beat far below, each
    roll echoing
around the cavern, reverberating, climbing up its sides.

"Thoom, thoom,": the deep slow heartbeat of the world.

Each stumbled step from rung to lower rung is a step into my
    history.

I have many shapes as I descend on my rope ladder. All
    distorted, ephemeral.
A twisted, stunted runt of me, projected on a granite shoulder
    rearing
from the night. A wild arm thinned into a jagged pencil line
    inching
up a cliff-side as my head drops down.

'Jerfal.' The word thrills me as it always does. She's here..
'Gribnocks.' She laughs when she hears me, a wraith of pleasure,
my arms outstretch towards her, the idea of her. She's
    somewhere
in the cavern, on her own rope ladder, but I don't know where.

No matter. We have our words to find, in turn..
'Yatterfail.'

'Dinch.'
'Millimangie.'

'Lesserwings.'
'Aridater.'
'Fooze.'

And so, as we descend towards the seat of the deep throbbing,
we dip into our reservoirs of words that might have been,
tie them in pale ribbon, float them to each other through the
  dark.

'Litterwinkles.'
'Mersery.'
'Glipponightshale.'
'Pote.'

She's sometimes to the left of me, sometimes to the right. I
  can't tell
if I'm spinning. I can only see three rungs, above me and
  below.

'Mellawrinkles.'
'Harthrough.'
'Kraptin.'
'Froo.'

The light changes below me, spurts of greyish-white, shifting
  mounds
of intense black. The deep throbbing remains. The air is
  warmer,
smells of sulphur. The dark is greenish. My foot, probing the
  darkness,
hits rock instead. I step off the ladder onto sand. I stretch
  behind me,
find her hand searching for mine. We clasp for a moment and
  let go.

The air seems fidgety, and now we've extinguished our candles
    we see
that it's populated with faint shapes, more shadow than
    substance,
large and slow, imbued with a kind of benign gravitas.

We look at each other. No words are needed.
Something ancient is about to be performed. We settle back in
    the warm sand.

The Attendance Register

Miss MacKenzie barked our names out. *Yessmiss!*
But there never was an answer from a girl
I didn't know, Wendy, Wendy Eva,
and purple silence stretched, thinned into violet,
chilling me each morning at 9.15am, for months.
Until one day – it was snowing – our teacher
rapped her ruler on the board, snapped out:
Wendy's agony is over. So you all must thank
the Lord for the mercy He has shown. By then
she'd become a haunting figure in my dreams,
and remains so, after more than sixty years.
She's here tonight, somewhere, swirling,
I think this is the only time we'll meet.

Light is dimmest at the conga's tail,
the dancers reduced to half-smiles, blemishes,
a pair of toenails, an earnest chin, and I find
not Bill Bazley but his hazel eyes,
he's pared down hugely, yet every bit as real.

Laughter warm enough for baking bread, notes
of a flute played under water. Searching
for a girl I never knew except by name,
who willed herself to thin to nothingness.

Breeze that calmed me on my first day at school,
a promise Amy tucked into her inkwell.
Scent of creosote down Howey Lane,
a chipped old marble I named *Wounded*,
bluebell-grove at the beginning of my world.

Floating past me is the Chinese burn
that Jake gave Brenda Barley
when she wouldn't share her plum.

Conga swallowing its tail. And there she is:
Wendy, twirling her umbrella, kicking higher
than I've ever seen before. She beckons me.
I feel her weight at last. The music holds its breath.

She turns to me. No eyes or mouth. She tastes of salt.

Transatlantic Connection

I don't recognise his newly broken voice,
distant, calm, no trace of the passion
in every word his father spoke.

He, who'd be so proud now if he knew
of the prizes, all across the board,
won by his phlegmatic son

who doesn't shy from praise
but accepts it
as if it were a biscuit or a frown

who answers all my questions, no facts
held back, yet nothing
to help me know him well: the son

of a man whose emotions ran so high
they caused chaos
and finally destroyed him

but the boy, today, remains unreachable
until I ask if I should send him
words his father spoke, aged eight,

which had found their way into a book.
Please send them! Yes!, voice breaking.
Now I can love him more – and fear for him.

Bodily

He's slumped on the settee, eyes closed.
I kneel between his thighs,
pushing on his heart,
sometimes thumping it,
intoning through the hour:
Come on now, Mike!
While his children,
not knowing, echo
as they romp around the room:
Come on now, Mike!
I know it's hopeless,
he's almost cold,
but I can't leave him
to reach room temperature alone.